The Magnificent Piano Recital

To Frank Graham, friend of my childhood,
on his 92nd birthday
M.R.

To Enrique Fernandez, who encouraged us
both in our artist endeavors.
L.F. & R.J.

The Magnificent Piano Recital

written by **Marilynn Reynolds**

illustrated by **Laura Fernandez & Rick Jacobson**

ORCA BOOK PUBLISHERS

ONE NIGHT in the middle of winter, a train blew its long whistle and threw on its brakes. It came to a stop at a sawmill town on the edge of a great northern lake. Out of the train came Arabella, her mother, two battered suitcases and a huge wooden crate. In the crate stood a piano.

In their cold bed that night, Mother and Arabella lay
cuddled together to keep warm. Mother wrapped her
arms around Arabella.

"I'm going to teach the children in this town to play
the piano," she whispered, "and when springtime comes,
we'll have a magnificent piano recital."

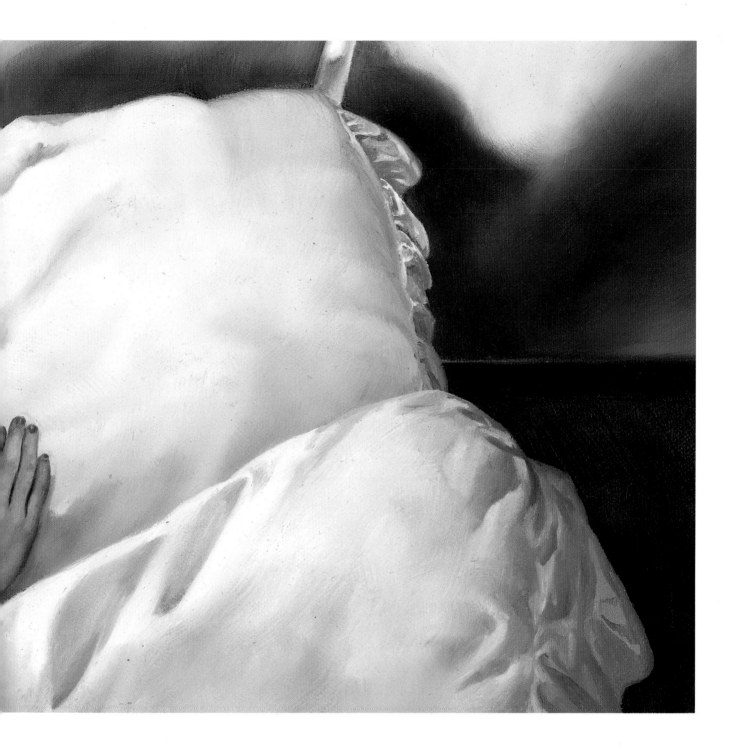

Arabella smiled as she thought of how wonderful the recital would be. Then Mother and Arabella fell asleep, as close together as two spoons.

In the morning Mother got up early. She took a sign from her suitcase and nailed it to their little house for the whole town to see: Aurora Jones, Piano Teacher.

On the kitchen wall near the stovepipe, Mother hammered in a big nail and hung on it a safety pin strung with Arabella's hair ribbons. The ribbons were purple, yellow, pink, blue, green, red, and white for best. Then Mother brushed Arabella's hair into ringlets.

"What color do you want to wear for your first day at school?"

Arabella had a cold. "Red," she answered, wiping her nose across her arm.

Mother tied a ribbon in Arabella's hair and buttoned up her dress with the frill around the bottom.

"I want to look nice to meet your new teacher too," Mother smiled. She pulled on her stockings with the seams up the back, her purple dress with the shoulder pads and her platform shoes with straps around the ankles. She opened the blue bottle of Evening in Paris perfume and rubbed some behind her ears.

It began to snow as Arabella and her mother walked hand in hand through the drifts and across the railway tracks to the town school.

The teacher stood at the door of the classroom. She looked at Mother's platform shoes with the straps around the ankles. She looked at the frill on Arabella's dress. She looked at Arabella's hair ribbon and her runny nose. She sniffed the Evening in Paris perfume.

"A-ra-bel-la." The teacher said the name as if it tasted bad in her mouth. "There's only one desk left," she added crossly, and she led Arabella to the back of the room.

The students turned around in their seats and stared. In the front row, the children were neatly dressed and their hair was smooth. Further back, the children were more shabby.

Mrs. Bat, for that was the teacher's name, marched to the top of the class. "Children shouldn't wear fancy party clothes and ribbons to school," she said. "And they shouldn't have their hair in ringlets." She clapped her hands sharply. "Eyes front! It's time for rhythm band."

Mrs. Bat carried a big box to the front row. She walked slowly past the desks, and the children chose their instruments. They picked out a silver triangle, tambourines like the ones the Gypsies played, bells on leather straps and black castanets that sounded like Spanish dancers. When at last Mrs. Bat came to her desk in the back, Arabella eagerly peered into the box. Only one thing was left — a pair of square wooden blocks.

"Hurry up," said Mrs. Bat. Then she marched to the front of the room and sat down at the piano. She banged a loud chord. "One, two, three!" she shouted, and the rhythm band began.

Bells jingled, castanets clicked, and tambourines rattled. High above the din, the silver triangle sang like a bird.

Arabella struck her blocks together. *Clunk, clunk, clunk*, they said dully.

Arabella's nose began to run. She put the blocks down and wiped her nose across her arm. Arabella knew that she would always be left with the blocks. She looked out the window at the snow falling on the black spruce trees in the schoolyard, and soon she didn't hear the rhythm band or the beautiful silver triangle.

When school was over, Arabella walked alone through the snow. It was colder than it had been in the morning and she shivered in last year's winter coat.

Her mother opened the door and hugged Arabella.

"How was school?" she asked.

"Fine," Arabella said.

When supper was over, Arabella sat at the piano and began to play. She played all the music Mother had taught her since she was small. She played until she forgot about the new school and the new teacher. She played until Mother kissed her cheek and told her that it was time for bed.

Early next morning Mother dressed Arabella for school. She hummed as she chose hair ribbons from the safety pin near the stovepipe and sang as she smoothed the ruffles on Arabella's dress.

After Arabella had trudged to school, Mother walked through the streets of town and nailed up posters about her piano lessons. Many people had pianos, but there had never been a piano teacher in town before.

Everyone stared at her hairdo, big earrings and strange shoes. "That's the new piano teacher," they whispered.

At first no one came to the little house for lessons. But one afternoon the owner of the sawmill brought his young daughter. Soon the banker's son came. And when they found out what a good teacher Mother was, many more parents brought their children to be taught.

Mother gave piano lessons at noon while Arabella sat alone at the kitchen table and ate canned spaghetti. She gave lessons at suppertime while Arabella ate pork and beans.

Once a week Arabella had her piano lesson, and sometimes, just for fun, they played a duet. Mother played the melody on the high notes while Arabella played the low notes, and their four hands moved together as though they belonged to one person.

And every night during the long winter, Arabella sat alone at the piano and played.

Spring came and the snow grew slushy. When Arabella walked home from school, she could smell the sap from the spruce trees mixed with the scent of wood dust from the sawmill, and she knew it would soon be time for the piano recital.

On the evening of the recital, Mother put on her new long black evening gown. She brushed her hair into an upsweep, like a movie star. Then she dabbed Evening in Paris behind her ears.

"Now tie this peplum for me," she said to Arabella. The peplum was covered with sequins and looked like a little apron. Carefully Arabella tied it around Mother's waist and made the best bow she could. Mother swirled around in front of the mirror.

"This will be a magnificent concert," she said, wrapping Arabella in a hug.

The stars were coming out as Mother and Arabella walked hand in hand across the railway tracks. The recital was held in a Quonset hut that looked like half of a giant moon sitting at the end of Main Street.

Everyone came to the first piano recital ever held in the town. The fat baker showed up with his tall skinny wife and their round little boy. The waitress who worked in the café hurried in after her shift was done. The banker with the moustache sat in the front row, and the cook from the hotel wore his old army uniform for the occasion. The tattooed truck drivers who hauled logs to the mill came in their plaid shirts. The Finnish lumbermen brought their tall blonde girlfriends. Proud mothers and fathers of the piano students arrived in their best clothes. And the owner of the sawmill came to the recital with his wife, who was wearing a diamond as big as a light bulb.

Even Mrs. Bat came. She sat in the middle with her purse on her lap and a sensible string of pearls around her neck.

Soon every chair was taken, and the Quonset hut buzzed like a hive of bees.

The whispering stopped when Mother stepped onto the stage. She was beautiful. The platform shoes made her look tall, and the lights on the ceiling glittered on her rhinestone earrings and on the shiny black sequins that dotted her peplum.

Mother welcomed everyone, and the piano recital began.

First came the banker's son. He played with his right hand only, carefully lifting each finger. The bigger pupils came next, playing some notes with their right hands and some notes with their left. The biggest children played with both hands. The audience clapped for a long time after each piece.

Finally it was Arabella's turn. Her shoes clicked loudly and her knees trembled as she walked across the stage to the piano.

"That's the teacher's little girl," she could hear someone whisper.

Arabella held her curved hands over the keys. She waited until the hall was very quiet, just as Mother had taught her. Then she began to play.

As first her fingers shook and she played stiffly. But soon she forgot all about the people in the audience. She thought only about her music. The music soared out of the piano and floated above the loggers and the truck drivers and the parents. The music flew around the walls and up to the highest arch of the Quonset hut, where it danced and sang before it grew softer and swept gently back into the piano.

Arabella played the final notes. Her fingers stayed on the keys until the music faded away. She lifted her hands from the keyboard, and only then did she remember where she was.

There was stunned silence. Then the Quonset hut burst into applause. The truck drivers waved their tattooed arms and stomped their big boots. The lumbermen cheered. The waitress hollered, "More! More!" The fat baker and the cook from the hotel shouted, "Encore!" And the mill owner's wife clapped until her diamond flashed like a thousand fireflies.

In the middle row, Mrs. Bat gasped with surprise at Arabella's music. She stared at the cheering people around her. When the audience got to its feet for a standing ovation, Mrs. Bat put her purse on the floor, stood up and clapped so hard, her sensible pearls shook.

Mother sat down on the piano bench beside Arabella.

"Let's play our duet for an encore," she whispered. "One, two, three." And up and down the keyboard they played, their four hands moving together as though they belonged to one person.

When the duet ended and the applause stopped, the smallest pupil came back onstage and presented Mother with twelve paper roses. Mother held the roses against her arm like an opera singer and curtseyed right down to the floor.

"Thank you for coming to our piano recital," she said as the lights sparkled on her rhinestone earrings and on the black sequins that dotted her peplum.

When Arabella slipped into her desk at school the next morning, she heard the children talking about the piano recital.

The freckled, red-headed girl who sat beside her whispered, "You played really good last night. Let's walk home together after school."

At the front of the room, Mrs. Bat clapped her hands for silence. "Quiet, everyone," she said. "It's time for rhythm band." She got out the box of instruments. Then she stopped and looked at everyone in the class, at the polished pupils in the front row and the shabby pupils behind.

"Today we'll start at the back," she said at last. And Mrs. Bat walked straight to Arabella's desk at the back of the room and held out the box of rhythm band instruments.

Arabella looked into the box. She looked at the bells on the leather straps, at the black castanets that sounded like Spanish dancers, at the tambourines like the ones the Gypsies played. She reached in and took the little triangle.

When all the children had chosen their instruments, Mrs. Bat shouted, "One, two three!" and banged the opening chords of the music.

The rhythm band rattled its song as spring sunshine poured in through the classroom window. Arabella looked around the room at the children. The freckled, red-headed girl gave her a big grin.

Then Arabella struck the triangle lightly. Its voice was high and clear and sounded like silver.

Canadian Cataloguing in Publication Data
Reynolds, Marilynn, 1940–
The magnificent piano recital

ISBN 1-55143-180-7

I. Fernandez, Laura. II. Jacobson, Rick. III. Title.
PS8585.E973M34 2000   jC813'.54   C99-911333-X   PZ7.R33732Ma 2000

First published in the United States, 2001

Library of Congress Catalog Card Number: 99-069237

Orca Book Publishers gratefully acknowledges the support for
our publishing programs provided by the following agencies:
The Government of Canada through the Book Publishing Industry
Development Program (BPIDP), The Canada Council for the Arts,
and the British Columbia Arts Council.

Cover design by Christine Toller
Printed and bound in Korea

IN CANADA: IN THE UNITED STATES:
Orca Book Publishers   Orca Book Publishers
PO Box 5626, Station B   PO Box 468
Victoria, BC Canada   Custer, WA   USA
V8R 6S4   98240-0468

02 00 00 • 5 4 3 2 1